PRAISE FOR MICHAEL BLOUIN:

FOR WORN DOWN TRUST:

"By times conversational and by times intensely, formally lyrical, *Wore Down Trust* explores masculinity, heartbreak, and the blues. Blouin uses a large canvas."
– MARILYN BOWERING & SUSAN MUSGRAVE

"The book is more than amazing. I find lines that stop me, lines I want to write down, wise lines, sad lines, funny lines... More than lines, a whole universe to be marvelled at here."
– SUSAN MUSGRAVE

"Watch out for *Wore Down Trust* by Michael Blouin."
– GEORGE FETHERLING

"Take a few consecutive hours out of your life, and read, in one sitting, a book that is compelling, insightful and thoroughly unconventional."
– NATIONAL POST

"Author Michael Blouin does a particularly remarkable job... effortlessly switching between poetry and prose.... This comes strongly recommended to the legitimately adventurous, those who enjoy not just reading manuscripts but climbing inside them, and examining the language found there much like kicking the tires of a used car. It is bound to be loved."
– CHICAGO CENTER FOR LITERATURE AND PHOTOGRAPHY

"Think of it as a daily devotional. You can pick it up, open it at random, read a few lines, stop, and then ponder the mysteries of life. Tomorrow and the next day, the experience can be repeated; a few more lines can be savoured."
– THE TELEGRAPH JOURNAL

"Creates vivid images revealed in the author's beautifully lean and powerful voice. Scores of vignettes are drawn together into a single, breathless tale of endurance, like water droplets coalescing into a dark pool. Buy it."
– NATIONAL POST

"Blouin's writing is like reportage from the edges, sharp-cutting sentences of no BS."
— MELANIE JANISSE

"Sorrowful, stirring pages."
— OTTAWA MAGAZINE

FOR CHASE & HAVEN:

"I love this book! It's very tender and beautifully written."
— LISA MOORE

"bill bisset likes *Chase and Haven* by Michael Blouin."
— bill bissett

FOR LET/LIE:

"*let\lie* will stay with you long after the close, and is well worth the fee for even just a handful of the gut-punching lines contained inside."
— BROKEN PENCIL

I DON'T KNOW HOW TO BEHAVE

A Fiction by Michael Blouin

BookThug · 2013

The production of this book was made possible through the generous assistance of the Canada Council for the Arts and the Ontario Arts Council.

Canada Council **Conseil des Arts**
for the Arts **du Canada**

ONTARIO ARTS COUNCIL
CONSEIL DES ARTS DE L'ONTARIO
50 YEARS OF ONTARIO GOVERNMENT SUPPORT OF THE ARTS
50 ANS DE SOUTIEN DU GOUVERNEMENT DE L'ONTARIO AUX ARTS

The Author would like to thank the Ontario Arts Council for a Works in Progress Grant which provided time to work on the writing of this book.

A complete list of sources is available from the publisher upon request.

LIBRARY AND ARCHIVES CANADA
CATALOGUING IN PUBLICATION

Blouin, Michael, 1960-, author
        I don't know how to behave : a fiction / Michael Blouin.

(Department of narrative studies ; 10)
Issued in print and electronic formats.
ISBN 978-1-927040-80-5 (PBK.). – ISBN 978-1-927040-91-1 (EPUB). –
ISBN 978-1-77166-024-2 (MOBI). – ISBN 978-1-77166-025-9 (PDF)

        1. Carter, Ken, 1938-1983 – Fiction. I. Title. II. Series:
Department of narrative studies ; 10

PS8603.L69I2 2013   C813'.6   C2013-905134-1
                                        C2013-905135-X

for my children; Tara, Taylor and Michaela:
never run from your demons – always follow your dreams

SOME
EPIGRAPHS

I took my love down to Summerstown
On the banks of the Seaway
Where the big ships go by
On the banks of the St. Lawrence River

we lie.

– DAVID FRANCEY AND MIKE FORD
 (*Banks of the Seaway,* 2009)

Humans are their own parables.

– GARY BARWIN, HUGH THOMAS, AND CRAIG CONLEY
 (*Franzlations: The Imaginary Kafka Parables,* 2011)

GTO: Those sons of bitches have been following me clear across two states. Three states. They keep wanting to challenge me. They come up behind and honk and then when I keep my cool and don't get into it they get hysterical. A bunch of small-town car freaks. They'd run over you if they had the chance. But that homemade stuff can't stand up to the old 455. I'd lose them in twenty minutes. Color me Gone, baby.

TEXAS HITCHHIKER: Well, I'll tell you one thing, you sure have one hell of a fast automobile.

– RUDOLPH WURLITZER AND WILL CORRY
 (*Two Lane Blacktop, A Screenplay*)

THE STORIES,
THE CHARACTERS,
THE SETTING

BOOK ONE

MIDNIGHT ALL NIGHT

Ken Carter was a Canadian daredevil who, in the 1970s, planned to jump a rocket-powered Lincoln Continental over the St. Lawrence River at Morrisburg, Ontario. Many of the events depicted here concerning his life are accurate. Not all.

BOOK TWO

HE GRABBED HER SUDDENLY, HELD HER
TO HIMSELF AND KISSED HER HARD
LIKE IN A HOLLYWOOD MOVIE

Bruce McDonald is an award-winning Canadian film and television director whose real life has (almost) nothing to do with the events depicted in this book. Bruce McDonald has never been indicted of racketeering or criminal conspiracy nor has any warrant ever been issued for his arrest.

Gillian Sze is a Canadian poet. She is also a fictional character in this book. She has never robbed a bank but she is up for a fight if necessary.

Morrisburg is a real place. Things happen there. But not often.

A DEFINITION

DEATH WISH

n.

    1. *Psychiatry*

        a. A desire for self-destruction, often accompanied by feelings of depression, hopelessness, and self-reproach.

        b. The desire, often unconscious, for the death of another person, such as a parent, toward whom one has unconscious hostility.

    2. A suicidal urge thought to drive certain people to put themselves consistently into dangerous situations.

– AMERICAN HERITAGE ONLINE DICTIONARY

A NOTE FROM THE AUTHOR

At the top of each page you will find the ongoing narrative told in a variety of forms and alternating between the two aforementioned storylines every three pages or so. At the bottom of most pages you will find an all-out effort to stop

(support)

this narrative in its tracks

(this narrative with documentation and expansion)

also using a variety of forms.

The rest of this is up to you.

MID-
NIGHT
ALL
NIGHT

1

KEN CARTER

MORRISBURG, 1979

EXT. – DAY

there's more ways of getting lost than not having a map

fast chrome mirrored sun off

hard glint St. Lawrence waves a sudden skip in the clouds

this was always going to have a cost

careful

now uncareful

rain in the air my

grave will be unmarked.

The ramp and its runway were located in a field just west of Hanes Road, south of County Road 2 in Morrisburg, Ontario, Canada. The ramp has since been demolished, but the concrete runway still exists though it is overgrown.

You will not find it unless you know it's there.

don't

like to be alone but sometimes I'm happier that way

no one expecting something to happen then

but there's the crowds too gathering like a Friday night jump at the track smouldering with just the smell of popcorn and beer and the spinning rubber blue exhaust

motel sign clicks off

lit cigarette burnt

out.

Carter was born in Montreal and grew up in a working-class neighborhood. With little education, he dropped out of school to perform car stunts with a team of travelling daredevils.

Soon he was a solo act.

thin line there at the top of the ramp

after that nothing

everything

spinning up

down

yellow scrub grass up under my feet cattail shimmer sun

you work for your dream or you fade but either way

bones in a box.

He jumped at racetracks all over North America and became a notorious showman, earning the nickname "The Mad Canadian" for his

death-defying antics.

HE GRABBED HER SUDDENLY, HELD HER TO HIMSELF AND KISSED HER HARD LIKE IN A HOLLYWOOD MOVIE

1

BRUCE MCDONALD

MORRISBURG, 1999

driving blind Port Hope Bancroft Coburg Brockville Morrisburg

the tall grass here hides everything

snow covers

the rest

most of the goddamned time

station drift dust sun and empty cups on the dash and next trip you drive

midnight-black Dodge Charger

goddamned Toronto skyscrapers and the rest of it behind

paper bag slides the length of faded dash milk smear windshield

you drive some

you stretch those long legs like that – I want everything you've got.

For Canada, moving pictures arrived on 28 June, 1896, in a former shooting gallery on rue de la Lagauchetière in downtown Montreal. From the fall of 1896, the movies appeared in various Canadian cities, as travelling showmen often brought to eager audiences a string of ten spectacles lasting one to five minutes.

"Do you think I've got them figured right?"

"Honey you've got them figured alright."

"Howso Rocket?"

"Because you know exactly where they live – corner of money and gimme some."

"That's their deal, it's always the money."

"That's their deal."

"Well…"

He takes a swipe at the condensation on the window. Pulls the blind down.

"Too much bright in here."

"Well what do you want to do… now?"

She smiles. She always smiles first. She kicks off her shoes. Skin extra light in the dim light. Pulls the socks slow. Orange peels on the floor. Casino eyes.

A few years ago he started writing a book. A novel. It started like this:

"She told me to get in the car. She didn't tell me where we were going. And we never got there."

He never got much further than that. Decided instead to go into the movie business. Told her there was a gun in the trunk. There was. He called her "Rocket." 'Cause she went off like one.

He read once somewhere this thing about a sociopath – if a sociopath was to come across a fatal car accident, and there was a dead child, and the mother was inconsolable, and if the mother were on her knees in the glass and blood, crying, screaming, the sociopath, he'd go home. And he'd practice making those same faces in the mirror.

Piece of information like that'd stop the earth in its tracks, he thinks. Fair scene in a movie, right there.

After dusk he wanders into the tree line behind the soft vinyl-sided building slowly driven by something he does not know, fingers lightly brushing the rough tree edges

his neck becomes sore from looking up

no stars.

The first Canadian films were produced in the fall of 1897, a year after the first public exhibition of motion pictures on 27 June, 1896, in Montreal. They were made by James Freer, a Manitoba farmer, and depicted life on the Prairies. The most successful producer was Ernest Shipman, who had already established his reputation as a promoter in the US when he returned to Canada in 1919 to produce Back to God's Country *in Calgary. This romantic adventure story of an embattled heroine triumphing over villainy was released worldwide and returned a 300% profit to its Calgary backers. During the next three years Shipman established companies in several Canadian cities and made six more features based on Canadian novels and filmed not in studios, as was then common, but on location. Though these films were not as profitable as his first, they were not failures. Only his last film,* Blue Water *(1923), made in New Brunswick, was a disaster. Shipman left Canada and died in 1931 in relative obscurity.*

MID-NIGHT ALL NIGHT

2

KEN CARTER

MONTREAL, 1976

a lot of what gets said isn't true
some things become more true over time
this place grew me

I remember us kids'd fight to be the one to be able to look through this
window... real fights, oh yeah
just to look out to that rust dirty bridge, the lit up cross

the bunk beds were over there
I knew there was a way out
this wallpaper still here see

real
in the winter when there was no heat I held the bars of the bunk bed
my freezing body shook.

*Fifteen forty-four Guy Avenue, Montreal. "Boy, this... you talk about searchin'
the memory banks. This really does it. It hasn't changed all that much. I don't
think it ever will."*

light falls the right way and I'm handsome

I'm Warren Oates on the screen maybe he could play me

he's always the one standing next to someone else in the movie

but hey

that's goddamned Warren Beatty he's standing next to

or Paul Newman

but I had this dream last night I was living on the side of this cliff I mean a
big one and I was making spaghetti there was a storm I think and far below
I'm looking out the window hundreds of feet below and cars are skidding off
the road and into these lakes or pools you know sometimes in dreams how
you can see so clear at a distance and these cars are sinking like pinpoints of
light into the dark water swallowed up and people are swimming to shore and
struggling to survive and I just want to have my spaghetti and I make myself
look away and it bothers me though you know because that's not who I am
I wouldn't do that I'd be scrambling down that cliff to help so why would I
dream that? I don't even like spaghetti.

*There were women, yeah. There were always women but there were always cars
too. Not enough time for both ever.*

I wanted to let you know this
that week you were gone
did things I haven't done in a long time
left the door...
unlocked all night

ate what was left of that skinned pudding straight from the bowl
cold chocolate
bare feet paled in the light from the fridge
wasn't sure you'd come back
just...
I didn't know... all the women I've loved... I've tried not to

you get what you get
but we can have anything we want
I believe that
in today's world, anything

steaks chops lunch dinner
Italian Chinese Canadian Cuisine
the sign says.

*Times he'd just sit looking out over all that choppy water. There was a lot of it.
That other shore was a far way off. I think he thought about that a lot.*

HE GRABBED HER SUDDENLY, HELD HER TO HIMSELF AND KISSED HER HARD LIKE IN A HOLLYWOOD MOVIE

2

BRUCE MCDONALD

MORRISBURG, 1999

"Tell your momma, tell your Pa...
I'm gonna send you back to Arkansas"
he'd always play that line twice for her
only played Ray Charles and Beethoven for her
only had the two cassettes

"How the hell is it you're from Winnipeg anyway?" he'd ask her
"They have Asians in Winnipeg you know," she'd say
"They got one less now."
Then she'd click her gum at him
"Everybody likes Chinese food."

In 1898, the Canadian Pacific Railway hired Manitoban James S. Freer to tour Britain with his realistic films of life in the Canadian West, in order to attract immigrants. These silent films were exhibited in community halls or similar venues in the United Kingdom with a knowledgable commentator at each performance. In 1902–03, the CPR engaged British producer/distributor Charles Urban, whose Bioscope Company of Canada shot promotional films, also to lure prospective immigrants to Canada.

beige plastic push-button phone the red button for messages and there's a freighter on the river now

"I know."

His eyes on the freighter over sunglasses. Adjusts the curtain now against the hard bouncing light.

"Yeah sure I do."
"I know about all that, the National Film Board made a documentary about it while it was happening. Took years, so what?"
"Because that's not the movie we're making. Do you know anything about history? It repeats itself. You learn from it."
"Well nobody's seen that movie. The movie we're going to make'll have people lined up around the block, two-deep."
"Because I know, that's how I know."

Lights up a smoke.

"Yup."

Smiles.

"People'll sell their dogs to get money to buy tickets to this fucking show."
"Okay. I am. Okay. Paul, Paul, stop thinking."
"Right."

Hangs up phone.

"Sell their dogs?" she asks from the bed.
"Fuck off."

Called scenics, the Living Canada films characteristically featured Canada au naturel, a vast untamed landscape that offered bounteous opportunity to those who seized it. The results were encouraging.

up all night forever when you're twelve and wondering and can't imagine yet eyes huge unquestioning but mind no not accepting how big it all could be but not yet not yet hands reaching silver up for something not there yet you're twelve you see you're pale and cold and sweating and you don't know yet that it could all be shit and there's still a chance yet that it might not

all

be

shit

in the night years later say the name of it with your rouged lips leaning heavy over me say the name of it

now say it now.

To deflect the widely held opinion that Canada was a land of ice and snow, the CPR had ordered winter scenes cut from its films. The Grand Trunk Railway Company tried its hand at these kinds of films too. Other producers like the Edison Company and Biograph, along with many small operators, continued to make actuality films featuring Canadian landscapes. Promotional films demonstrated primary production in lumbering, fishing, and mining. American producers tried their hand at shooting fictional films in Canada. They found the lowest common denominator worked best: stories often featured a villain.

MID-
NIGHT
ALL
NIGHT

3

KEN CARTER

MORRISBURG, 1979

I mean we all have something to give to the world

right?

does it ever occur to you, I mean if you stop, for a minute,

if you think about it all

I'm asking for a definition here

what do you think a junkie is?

Construction begins on some farmland near Morrisburg, Ontario, across the seaway from upstate New York. Fifty acres are cleared to make way for a 1,400-foot long take-off ramp, which would rise to 85 feet atop a massive earthen mound. Carter anticipates a live audience of 100,000. Constant rain mires tractors in the mud and otherwise hampers construction, and the rocket car isn't completed by the deadline.

In the early Spring of 1977, Carter visits the National Film Board labs in Montreal to watch some rough footage for the documentary shot the previous Fall. There's no sound with the raw footage he sees, though it was recorded the day of shooting and will be included in the finished film. The handheld shots show him making his way through the apartment building he grew up in, now abandoned.

"See I'm looking for something there."

"Wonder what it is I'm looking for."

On the screen he stands in the empty bedroom he had shared with his brothers.

"C'mon Carter, say something for the people."

Grins.

Produced by the National Film Board of Canada, The Devil at Your Heels *won the Genie Award for Best Theatrical Documentary. The title song was performed by bluesman "Long John" Baldry.*

not everything is going to go the way that you plan

I know that

welcome to life as they say

but you don't just lie down

all kinds of coffins and the holes to put 'em into

met that guy from the National Film Board he's a sharp tack

a sharp tack

and that's what you need

somebody itching for a kill.

The film was originally intended as a short on the jump attempt in 1975. Filmmaker Robert Fortier thought it would all take place over a couple of weeks, and he would get some great stunt footage. As things dragged on, he had to alter his plans.

my father said that he hated drinking
which is why he was trying to rid the world of rye I guess
one glass after another

he hit the road
never got anywhere worth being
that I know.

The documentary opens with some quick framing of the task, including footage of the ramp and the car to be used for the jump, and then chronicles how Ken Carter got his start as a daredevil, including footage of some early jumps. It then follows the ups and downs he experiences in his five-year journey to jump the river. He has a series of financial and technical obstacles. Technical problems include difficulties with the car (the fuel tank keeps blowing up) and the ramp he's planning to jump off (it's bumpy and not necessarily structurally sound). The financial problems are simpler; he keeps running out of money.

HE GRABBED HER SUDDENLY, HELD HER TO HIMSELF AND KISSED HER HARD LIKE IN A HOLLYWOOD MOVIE

3

BRUCE MCDONALD

MORRISBURG, 1999

they were making love

this is what we
come here to do he thinks
not this room

he means this planet
this life

his thoughts after that lost in the roar of her shower.

The villain was often a sex-starved French Canadian wilderness man, or a "half-breed" or a desperado on the run, lusting after the virtuous daughter of the Hudson's Bay post prefect or mounted police officer. All would be saved in the nick of time after the obligatory chase and rescue. This device, used early in Edwin S. Porter's The Great Train Robbery, *and repeated ceaselessly, became the mainstay of what would later be called Hollywood's Canada. These short films did much to condition the world's impression of what was alleged to be essentially Canadian. Unfortunately, they were universally inaccurate.*

they're like two people sitting on the edge of a bomb crater
like
everything just blew up and they're in shock

you can still smell the smoke in the air

The charm of the garden, he thinks. Her feet then in thin sheets stretched.
Colour T V in Every Room. Coffee cold. Twists the flesh on his arm to examine
it. Red. Too much sun.

*The irony was that Canadian actors hardly ever contributed to this distorted
imagery. With its small population and few urban centres, no substantial theatrical or music hall tradition existed from which to draw talent. And when
talent emerged, it almost always went south of the border. The predominant
pattern became one in which an American company filmed these Canadian
stories on sets or on location in the United States.*

she's upset
is Rachel weeping for her children because they are not
what he says to her gets lost in the general noise of the restaurant
his lips moving no sound
he'll dub that in
later.

McDonald was born in Kingston, Ontario. He graduated from the film program at Ryerson University. His first movie was The Plunge Murderer, *followed by a feature-length zombie flick,* Our Glorious Dead, *made with his grandfather's Super-8 camera and shot on location at his Rexdale, Ontario high school, North Albion Collegiate. The film premiered in the school cafeteria and made $100.*

MID-
NIGHT
ALL
NIGHT

4

KEN CARTER

MORRISBURG, 1979

the hand of God
that's what makes the decisions
just try to control everything the best you can
then foot to the floor

and a picture in my pocket always
she might be my daughter might not
fog smudged in cold waves spray off the river would be her birthday
today.

*The actual stunt lasts 14 seconds, including the eight seconds it takes for the car
to shoot down the runway.*

don't realize
sure it's nice
have the kids come up to you looking for an autograph

I'm saying
it's great to be Ken Carter
I wish I was.

seems to me there's nothing simple about simple, if there was there wouldn't be
so much complicated in the way

it's funny
you spend so much time making sure no man takes anything from you
your job, a woman, whatever

in honesty most often it's just you giving something up
not someone taking it
at all

one night at the track
everyone has their transistors tuned in and you could hear it over the midway
boys in the bright white sports car you know that one?

her thin hands loose between her legs like that.

sheet metal'll peel off that damn car like takin' the top off a tuna can

HE GRABBED HER SUDDENLY, HELD HER TO HIMSELF AND KISSED HER HARD LIKE IN A HOLLYWOOD MOVIE

4

BRUCE MCDONALD

MORRISBURG, 1999

you work it long enough
this meditation bit
and it works

you become the space you occupy
essentially you disappear
helps a bit if you're stoned.

An early American success of this nature was William Devereaux's Northern Idyll which was produced by Twentieth Century Fox and told the story of a young Inuit woman's search through an arctic blizzard for her white lover, an employee of the Hudson's Bay Company, and their subsequent rescue by a team of huskies. The entire film was shot over the course of three days in an aircraft hangar outside of Winnipeg in July utilizing in excess of three hundred tons of artificial snow and several large fans.

red carpet doesn't change a thing
I suppose most people probably think so
think: must be nice to be him

I'm really just thinking: do I have time for a smoke?
Is this an open bar?
The beautiful young nervous woman I'm standing next to

needs a fix.

After graduating from Ryerson, McDonald spent several years in the Far North, returning to Toronto to produce his privately funded first commercial feature Traplines *which was screened only once at the now defunct Bloor Cinema. The film is not listed in any McDonald bio. The Toronto Star published an advertisement for the screening but no subsequent reviews or notices have been documented. Of the film, McDonald has said nothing, reportedly once leaving an interview when questioned about it.*

Kingston 1979
went into the public washroom down by the basin
pisser is taken so I'm standing there in the stall
a metal air vent in the wall
dust an inch thick on it easy
looking like a lunar landing site tiny astronauts jumping
over at the sink an older guy in a red ball cap says to me:
you look like you could be a swimmer
you got a swimmer's build
I look in the mirror
and all the fluorescent lights flicker out
I'm saying how could I not have been a filmmaker
after that shit?

excerpt from the Traplines *shooting script:*

EXT. FIELD - DAWN

Archer: When a man gives me something from the goodness of his heart... like you gave me that this morning, I remember it from the heart.

Trouble: I know. That's why I want you to keep that lighter.

Archer: You stole it?

Trouble: It belonged to that English kid we just buried over there. He willed that lighter to me for a favour I done him. Archer?

Archer: What?

Trouble: Before I pass on, I want to do something to be remembered by.

MID-
NIGHT
ALL
NIGHT

5

KEN CARTER

MORRISBURG, 1979

the bright off the car roof you know?
squeezes your head like a lemon

there's a picture of my mother and father back when we lived at the old apartment when we were all still together in the one place they're in the kitchen in black and white smiling my father's got that light blue work-shirt with his name stitched on it my mother with her black frame glasses fake pearls rough fabric dress looking like the hand of God couldn't pull them apart of course He didn't need to they did that to themselves but they're both of them smiling that day big teeth to the camera even when you leave the room they're still smiling

like that
when you're gone

this new rocket car the height of the roof pushes me down the wrong way squeezes my hip into the gearshift but man when she takes off boy you know you're goin' somewhere she's beautiful I don't care I'd drive that car if the driver's seat was a pointed stick if the steering wheel was on

fire.

people in the crowd they want to say there's the guy, there he is, he don't look crazy, he looks like you and me when you're doin' a ramp-to-ramp jump with a stock automobile you do not have control 'til you're back on the ground they come to see a man do it not to get hurt but to do it without gettin' hurt and that's the trick takin' off is easy it's the landing that counts

I used to tell my brother
every time my father left the room
let's make a run for it, I said

he never did.

If you are new to screenwriting, planning to write a screenplay or script of any kind, the good news is that writing in screenplay format is easier and more intuitive today than at any time since first the Lanier Word Processing Machine. Advances in screenwriting software now save the hours you would previously have spent learning how to write a professional screenplay. Hollywood format can now be allocated to polishing your plot, honing your dialogue, or learning screenplay structure. Some think screenplay writing is eclipsing the pursuit of the Great Novel but it certainly isn't any easier. At any rate the making of movies is a collaborative process which demands that those in screenwriting produce a document in a particular format, notation, and length called a 'script.'

What?
Eh?
God!
Didya see that?
Looks on their faces I mean didya see that?
No aaaahhh –
what?
No. What? Ramps worked perfect –
eh? Yeah
I just didn't know if it would or not is the thing you know I felt that jolt
you know?
Glen here take this –
where's Terry? Huh?
Ha ha ha Terry didya see?

Didya see their faces?
Love it   love it.

(1976 Jump, Cornwall Speedway, 17 cars)

In many cases the best screenplays will seem entirely unscripted such that the work of the writer fades into the background as it were and the dialogue takes centre stage. In genres such as cinéma-vérite scripted scenes may often seem off the cuff and scenes in which the actors seem to be adlibbing their lines may in fact have been carefully scripted. In any case it is the work of the screenwriter to place him or herself as far off the screen as possible.

HE GRABBED
HER SUDDENLY,
HELD HER TO
HIMSELF AND
KISSED HER
HARD LIKE IN A
HOLLYWOOD
MOVIE

5

BRUCE MCDONALD

MORRISBURG, 1999

EXT. – DAY

We are floating up a steep scrubby slope towards what appears to be a huge cement ramp leading nowhere. The camera moves haphazardly as if being carried by someone who has forgotten that it is there. We hear a voice gently singing "Tumbling Tumbleweeds" from a cheap distant speaker, a car radio, and a distinctive, affable, male voice – Bruce McDonald's, perhaps:

VOICE-OVER: This is it see? Right there. Not all of it. See? The car was meant to come right up here, take off the hell up that ramp, there was more of it then. Take off like a rocket.

We top the ramp and the vastness of the St. Lawrence River stretches out before us. Sun glints off the water and the camera turns back to the speaker's face.

BRUCE MCDONALD: They call Los Angeles the City of Angels. Paris the City of Lights. Morrisburg – that's the City of Dreams.

The camera pans back over the water and down river to the town of Morrisburg. (zoom, blur focus)

BRUCE: This is it, see? Right there. Not small-town Ontario like it looks. City of Dreams.

INT. – MCINTOSH COUNTRY INN – MORRISBURG

It is late, the room is dark save for the light from the television. We are tracking looking down over the bed where lie a fortyish man in boxer shorts and a young Asian woman in T-shirt and panties. They are asleep.

VOICE-OVER: Now this story I'm about to unfold…
Let's just say… it's personal.

This overview will begin to acquaint you with the screenplay format writing rules and screenwriting etiquette you'll need to know about.

GILLIAN: "You want some of this?"
BRUCE: "What?"
GILLIAN: "Toast."

BRUCE: "No."

GILLIAN: "I'm tired of this."
BRUCE: "What? Toast?"
GILLIAN: "Shit, I'm tired of all this shit."

BRUCE: "Whataya going to do about it?"

TABLE OF CONTENTS – CHAPTER ONE

skin like rice paper

and like water

scrunches her mouth together on one side when she thinks

like a schoolgirl or a killer

this is how she cries

which she doesn't do often or at all

really

she'll arrange things on the dresser arrange them again gaze silently into the mirror

her life weighs twenty-eight years, seven months, three days, fourteen hours and this minute, which feels particularly

heavy now

and there's thunder some girls get sad or hysterical some just get busy some get even for everything

she takes a picture the camera in her hands she likes to take pictures and the gun in the trunk she thinks about you can see that in her eyes, here, see?

MOTEL ROOM – INT. – DAY

(Gillian is slumped disconsolately back on the bed, fingers of one hand cupped over her sunglasses. Her other hand makes shadows on the wall.)

This overview will begin to acquaint you with the screenplay format, writing rules, and the screenwriting etiquette you'll need to know about. As you browse the following material, you may notice the words "don't," "avoid" and "unless you are directing the movie." Take that advice to heart. As you become more familiar with the world of screenwriting, you'll understand why, but for now, the scope of this document prohibits a deeper explanation.

MID-
NIGHT
ALL
NIGHT

6

KEN CARTER

MORRISBURG, 1979

Little victories, my mother used to say; that was her thing. Well, I don't know what she meant by that; maybe you don't win it all, you just win sometimes, but I'm not interested in that. Ken Carter has no time for thinking that he might not do something or I might not win because winners just think about winning and you don't win by losing a little bit at a time... The ultimate statement, "Ken Carter – World's Greatest Daredevil" that's what I'm after."

– *Devil at Your Heels,* 1981, 23:17

(and he runs his hand softly over the hood of the car)

The actual stunt lasts fourteen seconds, including the eight seconds it takes for the car to shoot down the runway and up the ramp and the six seconds it takes for it to float down to the water, its descent slowed by two parachutes, deployed early because, upon leaving the ramp, the car dissipates immediately into a spray of body panels, like a bird hit by buckshot.

let's be honest there've been some women involved
tell 'em they shouldn't love me but that's the thing about women
well, let's face it
there's lots of things about women
I came over here today because I said that I would
I didn't say I'd drink all this beer though

remember when Ronnie Talbot near died on that Detroit jump,
there was enough blood there for the end of a man that's for certain
I don't care to worry – it's not in me
I'd like to have flowers at my funeral though
and some shrimp cocktails
no speeches

and I'd like to learn something
from this life
there'll always be something to long for.

grav·i·ty noun /ˈgravitē/
     1. The force that attracts a body toward the centre of the earth, or toward any other physical body having mass.

if she comes out bad you just clamp those jumper cables onto me
and give'er the gas
no, you know, being serious though for a moment, a little bit too much push
on the pedal, one inch off on the line that you should be taking, you need to
take, or some water on the ramp, or the chutes don't open…
shoot, we got the best people on this I tell ya
that's why we're so careful
'cuz all it takes is a little thing
an inch wrong down here and you're three hundred feet off up there
that's it.

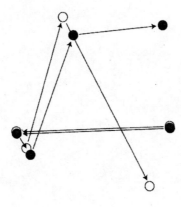

In chaos theory, the map defined by

$$x \to 4\,x\,(1 - x) \ and \ y \to x + y \ if \ x + y < 1 \ (x + y - 1 \ otherwise)$$

*displays sensitivity to initial conditions. Here, two series of x and y values
diverge markedly over time from a tiny initial difference.*

HE GRABBED HER SUDDENLY, HELD HER TO HIMSELF AND KISSED HER HARD LIKE IN A HOLLYWOOD MOVIE

6

BRUCE MCDONALD

MORRISBURG, 1999

robbing banks is easy – making movies is hard
but they're not unrelated
favourite rides are the dark ones
my favourite places have sticky floors

the sky is bright and the sun is shining – makes me uneasy.

excerpt from the Traplines *shooting script:*

INT. – BUNKER

Archer: "We just stopped that thing."
Trouble: "What was that called?"
Archer: "Armageddon."
Trouble: "That's the one."
Archer: "We just did what we needed to do."
Gillian: "With a sharp stick."

MORRISBURG LEADER INTERVIEW – OCTOBER 10, 1999:

Toronto film director Bruce McDonald is visiting Morrisburg and scouting locations for a film he says he intends to produce about the ill-fated 1979 "Super Jump" attempted over the St. Lawrence River just west of Morrisburg by daredevil Ken Carter. The Leader *caught up with him this week.*

ML: So how did you come to this idea for a project and why did the story of Ken Carter interest you?

BM: A friend of mine passed the video documentary on to me. I think I just fell in love with this crazy idea and with the man behind it. He was very driven and maybe a bit crazy (laughs) and, you know, very authentic in a way – so I thought, well, that's an interesting combination. Ken Carter, what he did, or tried to do, it's like a piece of folk art I think. I think that was what kind of captured my attention.

ML: This is a little different than the films you've done to date?

BM: Yeah. Well, I don't know. I like characters who pursue dreams which may not be what most people would choose – outsiders and outlaws. And people who aren't afraid to kind of go to a couple of dark places. So I think it was that kind of feeling that drew me to this story. I like the idea of working with history – manipulating it as a material.

ML: It's not a very well-known story – outside of locally anyway.

BM: Sometimes history gets tossed aside and left behind – history often does not get noticed while it's being made; often in art, that's true anyway. And I think that in some ways what Carter was doing was art. I don't know that he'd see it that way.

ML: Not a lot of people around here liked him much, you know.

BM: Not a lot of people like me.

ML: They found him a little arrogant.

BM: That's the way they find me too.

G: You got that right.

excerpt from the Traplines *shooting script:*

INT. – BUNKER

Archer: Who did you say you were?
Reporter 1: I didn't. I'm a reporter.
Archer: Shoot this one!

Gillian takes a picture of the highway outside the motel

of the mailbox in the cold

of the woman in the red sweater pulled close on the porch the white clapboard behind her

you understand what I'm saying – all of these pictures she takes are very, very good – it is the best possible picture of the highway outside this motel anyone could take, possibly the best mailbox picture ever taken by anyone, each of these pictures could be a poster, the cover of a record, cover of a book… But what she wants, the reason she keeps taking them, she wants a picture like a throat punch, she wants a picture like the one taken five minutes after the head-on collision, taken right through the windshield, the one the newspaper won't publish, "what are you thinking ferchristsake this is a family newspaper you gonna pay for that lawsuit you gonna answer those phone calls?" She wants a picture like the splash of rye to the back of the throat, like a powder keg, the sudden gun to the back of the head the cold steel circle

seldom really satisfied

is

she'll leave. she knows. he knows. she will.

MID-
NIGHT
ALL
NIGHT

7

KEN CARTER

MORRISBURG, 1979

I was right next to a freight train that jumped the tracks once
I don't mean after
I mean while

one hand up to block the sparks
the other to stop the train
if necessary

I talk like I understand
I walk like
I·have somewhere to go.

"In the old days they, the promoters, wanted more and more from me. They wanted me to jump or spill my blood and break my bones. Every time they wanted me to jump further, and further, and further. Hell, they thought my bike had wings. I forget all of the things that have broke."

– Evel Knievel

nothing in hell would ever get done if you waited around until you felt just right about it

EXT. – ONTARIO MOTOR SPEEDWAY – ONTARIO, CALIFORNIA

Evel Knievel is speaking directly to the camera describing his upcoming daredevil motorcycle jump:

KNIEVEL:

Ladies and gentlemen, you have no idea how good it makes me feel to be here today. It is truly an honour to risk my life for you. An honour. Before I jump this motorcycle over these ninteen cars – and I want you to know there's not a Volkswagen or a Datsun in the row – before I sail cleanly over that last truck, I want to tell you that last night a kid came up to me and he said, "Mr. Knievel, are you crazy? That jump you're going to make is impossible, but I already have my tickets because I want to see you splatter." That's right, that's what he said. And I told that boy last night that nothing is impossible.

don't know how to give up on a dream 'course I don't hope I never find out.

LONG SHOT – EXT. DAY – EVEL KNIEVEL AS A BOY WALKS IN
A DESERT LANSCAPE, A MOUNTAIN RANGE BEHIND HIM. HE
IS INTENT UPON THE YO-YO DANGLING FROM HIS FINGERS

KNIEVEL – VOICE-OVER:

Butte, Montana was a mean place to grow up in. For one thing,
the mountain behind Butte and the ground underneath it were
completely honeycombed with mineshafts. You could expect any
day for the whole place just to fall into the earth and disappear
like the lost world of Atlantis.

(A beat-up car appears behind Knievel and drives toward him.
He is unperturbed and continues to play with his Yo-Yo.)

There was not a safe place to stand.

(The car comes to a stop behind Knievel, who is blocking the
road, and honks its horn. He continues to play with his Yo-Yo,

the driver waves at him to move. Suddenly the car falls through the ground, completely disappearing from view. The sound of the horn diminishes, the dust clears, Knievel winds up his Yo-Yo, steps forward and peers down the hole, the sound of the horn becoming ever fainter.)

Well, it is no wonder I became a wild man, living in a place like that.

EXT. DAY – CROWD IN BLEACHERS – THE YOUNG KNIEVEL SITS NEXT TO HIS MOTHER

KNIEVEL – VOICE-OVER:

I saw my first daredevil show at the age of twelve. One fellow blew himself up with dynamite and another got pinned and spread across a retaining wall, smashed all over the place. Mother enjoyed this show a great deal and so did my brother, who said it was very interesting but he could take it or leave it. I found it to be a very moving experience.

HE GRABBED
HER SUDDENLY,
HELD HER TO
HIMSELF AND
KISSED HER
HARD LIKE IN A
HOLLYWOOD
MOVIE

7

GILLIAN SZE

MORRISBURG, 1999

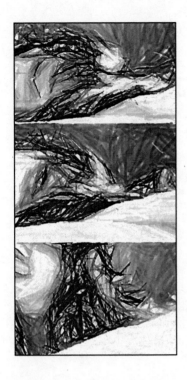

BRUCE: "I want you to do the storyboards for this film."

GILLIAN: "Why?"

BRUCE: "Because you can draw. And you're here. And what else do you have to do?"

GILLIAN: "You say sweet things."

BRUCE: "What's wrong with you?"

GILLIAN: "You."

Storyboards are graphic organizers, such as a series of illustrations or images displayed in sequence for the purpose of pre-visualizing a motion picture, animation, motion graphic or interactive media sequence, including website interactivity. The storyboarding process, in the form it is known today, was developed at the Walt Disney Studio during the early 1930s, after several years of similar processes being in use at Walt Disney and other animation studios.

BRUCE: "You remember that drawing you did of me once?"

GILLIAN: "No."

BRUCE: "Yes you do, in Montreal; I liked that one. I want storyboard pictures like that."

GILLIAN: "That's nice."

BRUCE: "Well?"

GILLIAN: "Well, get yourself some charcoal."

BRUCE: "Where is that drawing you did of me?"

GILLIAN: "—"

Storyboards are now becoming more popular with novelists. Because most novelists write their stories by scenes rather than chapters, storyboards are useful for plotting the story in a sequence of events and rearranging the scenes accordingly.

BRUCE: "That doesn't hurt me you know, you not talking to me."

(Gillian exits, taking her drawing pad into the washroom, and closing the door.)

INT. BATHROOM - NIGHT

With the water running she draws late into the night under the stark fluorescent light, seated on the tile floor with her knees drawn up. Montage of shots. Close-ups. Hands. The tap drips. Eyes. Lips compressed. Focus. This scene is called "Self-portrait."

MID-
NIGHT
ALL
NIGHT

8

KEN CARTER

MORRISBURG, 1979

there are two things I remember happening to me when I was, I don't know, maybe ten years old: the first was my mother took me to the Orange Julep out Decarie Boulevard; you know, there's a big orange and you go up to this little window and you buy your drink, well there was a bell on the counter that you ring for service, you know, to get your drink, to get the fella to come and make it, and I just kept ringing and ringing that little bell and the fella comes out of the back and boy I'll tell ya he must have been all kinds of pissed off and he looks and sees it's just me just a kid and he says kid you like that bell and I said, I don't know, I suppose I said yes sir and he says to me you can have it and says to my mother take it home for him lady the other thing is she took me to see Blackstone the Magician at the Seville Theatre on Sainte-Catherine Street and I wore this red shirt I had and Blackstone he called me up onto the stage probably spotted me because of that shirt and he asked me if I could have a rabbit what would I name it and I couldn't think of any name to say and he said to me so no one else could hear it, "Ask if it's a boy or a girl rabbit" like he was a ventriloquist I mean you couldn't see his mouth move at all and when I said it like I thought of it myself all the people laughed and then he made this rabbit appear out of a rolled-up newspaper now I don't know how he did it and I learned two things out of these two experiences first, you gotta be persistent and second, the people, they want to be impressed

and wearing a nice shirt – that doesn't hurt either.

Suspension of disbelief or "willing suspension of disbelief" is a formula for justifying the use of fantastic or non-realistic elements in literary works of fiction.

See even when I was that young I began to realize that there is no point in being here being anywhere if you're not one of the ones making a difference in this world having an effect doing something and those people who work nine to five in some factory, and I've done that, and they go out on a Friday or on a Saturday night and they want to be entertained, and they should be entertained, and whether that's by Frank Sinatra or by The Eagles like they sing teach your children or by some guy like me jumping a car over ten, eleven, twenty other cars and maybe breakin' his neck or his leg or dyin' in front of them that's what they get and they paid for their ticket and that's all. This is what I think these are my thoughts as I'm thinking them Ken Carter, Kenneth Gordon Polsjek, you get that? Camera's on? So that's what I think – people deserve to have their dreams.

– *Devil at Your Heels*, 1981, 23:17

It was put forth in English by the poet and aesthetic philosopher Samuel Taylor Coleridge, who suggested that if a writer could infuse a "human interest and a semblance of truth" into a fantastic tale, the reader would suspend judgment concerning the implausibility of the narrative. Suspension of disbelief often applies to fictional works of the action, comedy, and horror genres.

lost something comin' down the back end there

huh? I don't know

I could smell the fuel line open up and

what? lost the back end completely, yeah, and the headlights cut out too, electrical maybe

thought I smelled fire.

In 1983, Carter attempted to jump a pond in Peterborough, Ontario. During the jump, his car – a modified Pontiac Firebird – had a malfunction and Carter crashed badly but vowed to try the jump again. Several months later he did.

A distinctive, slant-nose facelift occurred in 1977, redone somewhat in 1979. From 1977 to 1981, the Firebird used four square headlamps, while the Camaro continued to retain the two round headlights that had previously been shared by both Second Generation designs. Curb weights rose dramatically in the 1973 model year due to the implementation of 5 mph (8 km/h) telescoping bumpers and various other crash and safety related structural enhancements.

HE GRABBED HER SUDDENLY, HELD HER TO HIMSELF AND KISSED HER HARD LIKE IN A HOLLYWOOD MOVIE

8

BRUCE MCDONALD

MORRISBURG, 1999

Gimme a Jack and Dry on ice again. The shit of it is that I love her. Yeah. Yep. Well. All women want to hear that they're loved I'm well aware of that but that does not mean that they want to hear it from me. There's too many that's in that line. Be hard for an actor to get out of a line like that without tripping up on it along the way. The way she wakes up in the morning and she greets the day do you know what I mean? I mean other people they just try to get up or they bitch and moan about getting up. She is aware of the light in the room. I'm saying that she interacts with the light in the room. Like she absorbs it – it soaks into her. And this is before she even gets out of the bed. She is like a fucking plant or something. She's like someone who belongs on this planet, you know what I mean? Not this fucked-up planet we've – this planet like if it was all just water and air and green again and she'd look like she belonged on it. Not like me, or you, we'd all be looking for our shoes or a grocery store or a bar. She would just be there. Just be there in the sun like she just woke up in her bed. What I mean… I watch what happens. She is what happens. You see the difference? Shit. You and me we can sit in a room. She

(opens hands in front of face like he's producing flowers out of thin air)

occupies the room.

(laughs, looks at glass, looks up)

She's the fucking reason the light came in. The rest of the world wants to be part of her – you see what I'm saying? The light wants to be on her – it's just what I said. She's like a plant or a fucking tree. She's integral. She's integrated.

She is the space that she occupies, and she's this little extra space around that. Like this extra light that she has. An extra share. You ever seen her dancing next to a record machine, you'd know what I mean. She's the fucking reason the light came in the room. I can't compete with that. I'm a deck of cards in her ass pocket.

Let me tell you this: I once went on a trip to the ocean, just me and this couple I know and their kid. We drove an old rusted Rambler out to the beach with a fucking picnic blanket, you know? We get to the ocean and their kid, he's six years old; it's the first time he's ever seen the ocean, right? The kid is six years old and it's the first time he's ever seen the ocean and we're standing there with our shoes off. The waves are coming in. Kid says:

"It's not so great."

Fucking genius. Look, I've been looking at it all my life, and you know what? It's not that great. Kid saw it real the first time. I just put my fucking shoes back on and went back to the car.

But now, you put her there on that beach. Take her shoes off and let the salt water wash over her feet. Maybe make her laugh and hop up and down a little… Now my friend, now you've got something. Water's got a reason to be there now.

Even the fucking genius kid would see that. He'd see it clear. The shit of it is I couldn't even tell her this anyway. I didn't know how to get the line out.

I can't play pathos. And she wouldn't care.

"You are the reason the light came into the room."

(shakes head)

It's a crap line.

Nobody could pull that shit off.

I wouldn't ask 'em to. Besides.

I don't think she can stand me much anyway. I'd do better bein' a damn birdwatcher with a pair of binoculars. Or making my own homemade jam.

She's a country.

I'm a refugee.

The phrase "suspension of disbelief" came to be used more loosely in the later twentieth century, often used to imply that the onus was on the reader, rather than the writer, to achieve it. It might be used to refer to the willingness of the audience to overlook the limitations of a medium, so that these do not interfere with the acceptance of those premises. These fictional premises may also lend to the engagement of the mind and perhaps proposition of thoughts, ideas, art and theories.

the more she drew pictures of herself the better she got I'm saying the clearer she got

in her mind and on the paper

(but mostly in her mind)

by the time I left that bar I was in no condition to even walk you understand what I'm saying she found me on somebody's front lawn she pretty much carried me back to the motel

Rocket, I told her, someday they're gonna make a movie out of my life and you can be in it

Great, she said, ...Who's going to do the storyboards?

('bout then she decided to rob the bank. well. it was something to do with the gun.)

"This movie has all the answers."

– COMMENT ON AN ONLINE BULLETIN BOARD REGARDING
THE NATIONAL FILM BOARD'S KEN CARTER DOCUMENTARY

She storyboarded the most important things she did before she did them.

She drew herself coming in wearing the hood. Filling out the note. The last shot she drew was of her running up to the teller's counter pointing the gun as the teller punched the alarm. It went pretty smoothly. In the storyboard no one got shot.

MORRISBURG, 30 OCTOBER 1999, 10:07AM

MID-
NIGHT
ALL
NIGHT

9

KEN CARTER

MORRISBURG, 1979

So I've explained everything to the big money guys. One, two, three. I think they understand now. Wanted to tell them it's not rocket science but it is now, really. So I made it simple for them. There's no need in getting them mixed up with the details of rigging a modified Detroit Lincoln Continental with a hydrogen-fueled rocket engine. In the end all you do is strap yourself into it and hit the gas. The details are for the guys that you hire. So's the money because you have to hire the best. You better hire the best 'cause you're gonna be the beans in the can, you know what I mean? That's what I need the money for. To pay the guys that – it's like they're designing a very sharp stick see, and I'm either gonna ride it to success or it's gonna go right up my ass. Either way it's my ass. What I'm saying is it better not be a stick, it better be one hell of a good rocket car and it will be, it is, because this thing is gonna happen. We've got the best people on this. You see what I'm saying. I mean we have to.

1977 LINCOLN CONTINENTAL INFORMATION SUMMARY

Body: Sedan/saloon
Length: 5918 mm
Weight: 2222 kg
Engine Capacity: 7536 cc
Cylinders: V8
Maximum Power: 210.9 PS/208 bhp 155.1kW @ 4000 rpm
Maximum Torque: 482.0 NM/356 FT. LB/49.2 kgm @ 2000 rpm

honesty

you want to do something that is true and honest
not a worry in the world then
it's what I don't do and what I don't say that worries me
I risk myself
but I do it for a reason
people know they've seen a show
they got their money's worth
it's my need to carry on
that keeps me going
keeps them coming back I guess.

The awareness of cinema's potential to lie would result in filmmakers trying precise ways of shooting. For Michel Brault of the National Film Board of Canada, who pioneered modern hand-held camera work, it meant the ability to go amidst the people with a wide angle. Other filmmakers would develop different methods. Some insisted that their subject needed to get used to them before they started any real shooting, so it would seem the camera was being ignored.

song and dance always selling something to the public to the reporters to your backers to yourself always the same deal you're playing you got the straps on in the car and the wind is blowing I mean you know it's going to happen always the same thing car lifts off in one place lands in another always the same you're okay or you're not that's the way that it is that's it that's it.

Still another group of Direct Cinema filmmakers would claim that the most honest technique was for a filmmaker to accept the camera as a catalyst and acknowledge that it provoked reactions. This allowed filmmakers to feel free to ask their film subject to do something they would like to document. The filmmakers were then free to "influence" the action.

HE GRABBED
HER SUDDENLY,
HELD HER TO
HIMSELF AND
KISSED HER
HARD LIKE IN A
HOLLYWOOD
MOVIE

9

BRUCE MCDONALD

MORRISBURG, 1999

(at the hotel)

She's the triple threat: she writes – she draws – she takes pictures she's...
beautiful

That's four

(lights a match)

No I mean there's so much going on there but it's just there, you know, she
doesn't push anything at anyone she just does these incredible things quietly
sits up at night and writes these little poems on slips of paper from the hotel
memo pad

(Laughs)

And they're tremendous you know they're... real

(Pauses)

Really, something I've always admired – people who are writers – the ability to
get something down so someone believes it so you really believe it's happening
right now... but it's just in your head.

(lights a match)

(close-up)

BRUCE: "It's all in your head. Certain things can't be hidden though."

(drops match on carpet)

BRUCE: "Certain things are buried pretty deep down inside maybe but they'll
come out... given the right circumstances. But I'm not a betting man... Fuck
it."

The Hollywood film is an escape of one sort or another. But our films make it damn near impossible to escape. We're interested in what you can't escape from and presenting it... Some people get a little edgy when they see something that is so personal. They don't know where to turn to look for the kind of buffer that most movies give them. In fiction you can say 'it's only a movie' and forget it. You can't do that with reality.

— ALBERT MAYSLES TO *The New York Times*, 18 OCTOBER 1987

or you can sleep for a long time and still be tired
or you can stay up for a really long time and feel really awake
or you can live for a long time and feel tired all of the time
or just sit around thinking about things
or you can get off your perfectly formed ass and do
it right now

there is no other time. Wake up.

The Venus symbol is a depiction of a circle with a small cross below it. The symbol is historically associated with the Roman goddess Venus or the Greek goddess Aphrodite. It has a unicode designation of U+2640, and is used in various media to represent things associated in some way with mythological characters of the female sex and feminism in philosophy and sociology.

The symbol is also believed by some to represent a hand mirror, with the top half representing the actual mirror, and the bottom half representing the handle of the mirror.

MID-
NIGHT
ALL
NIGHT

10

KEN CARTER

MORRISBURG, 1979

or that car chase scene in that movie with Steve McQueen, *Bullitt*

you seen that? way they had that camera right in the car there with him

well that's what we're going to have here – reality

(spreads hands)

"You are there."

The National Observer said, "Whatever you have heard about the auto chase scene in Bullitt is probably true... a terrifying, deafening shocker." Life magazine wrote, "... A crime flick with a taste of genius... an action sequence that must be compared to the best in film history."

I mean that was one hell of a movie I mean that was a real show

Sheryl she always wanted to be a singer

I guess she is a singer now
last time I saw her we went to see that movie
I knew there was only room for one famous person in a marriage so that was
the end of that
pretty much she sings in Nova Scotia and I jump cars everywhere else

I liked the way her eyes lined up at the corners when she smiled
like she didn't want to smile but she couldn't help it
I made her laugh as often as I could though
some people they stick to you

sometimes I see her in a crowd

it's never her.

155P INT. – BULLITT'S MUSTANG SHOT THROUGH WINDSHIELD

He sees the Dodge speeding across the intersection, just as the
light changes to red. Bullitt accelerates with a burst of speed. As
he nears the intersection, a big truck starts to cross from the
right. Bullitt twists sharply, and just manages to get past the
truck by inches.

126

you are eventually worn down by everything that you know

sometimes it's just better not to carry too many facts with you

like in a war movie – they can't torture out of you what's not in there to begin
   with

I keep track of what I need to know

reporter asked me do you think this jump will generate much interest?

I said

You're here, aren't you?

INT. - BULLITT'S APARTMENT SATURDAY NIGHT

The telephone rings. Bullitt rolls over, grabs the phone.

HE GRABBED HER SUDDENLY, HELD HER TO HIMSELF AND KISSED HER HARD LIKE IN A HOLLYWOOD MOVIE

10

BRUCE MCDONALD AND GILLIAN SZE

MORRISBURG, 1999

INT. - MOTEL ROOM MORNING

BRUCE:

"Hello?"

BRUCE:

"What?"

(checks bed next to himself)

BRUCE:

Looks like she's not here. Yeah. Yeah I'm sure she did give you this number because this is her number, she's just not at it right now. Where is she? Just a sec, I'll ask her.

(pauses; holds the receiver up to the empty room; brings receiver back)

BRUCE:

Nope. Can't ask her, she's not here ... May I say who's calling? So when she returns I can tell her who called? What's that?

(reaches for a pen and paper; knocks ashtray off nightstand)

BRUCE:

Fuck. What? No I just ... Hold on.

(sits up in the bed; draws one hand down his face and lifts the receiver again)

BRUCE:

This is tiring me out. You got a name or number I can give her? You got any hot coffee? No? I could use a coffee. Okay, hold on.

(clicks pen)

BRUCE:

Jeff. Solar Films. Production Assistant job. New York, for five weeks. She have your number, Jeff? Starting when? Now. Now? Well, I think she may be very busy right now. At the moment. She's working on storyboards. Storyboards. She's an artist. She doesn't get people's fucking coffee and pick up people's fucking dry cleaning. Yeah, no, I understand. Well, I'll tell her. I will. Jeff. Yeah.

(hangs up; sits looking at the phone; lights a cigarette; reaches and forcibly pulls the phone cord out of the receiver, places the receiver back on its cradle, then touches it gently; rests back on the bed with one arm over his face)

BRUCE:

Jeff.

(sighs)

BRUCE:

Now I need my fucking phone fixed, Jeff.

DREAM SYMBOLS: PHONE

To use a phone in your dream represents a message or advice that comes with a price. It may also mean that your communication with others is having a toll on you in some way, either directly or indirectly.

To dream that the phone is out of order indicates that you are being shut out. You are experiencing difficulties in getting your thoughts and feelings across. Or you are having difficulties connecting with others.

 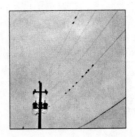

this morning takes on the shape of a body outline in chalk on the grey pavement cold rain washing this morning is the shape of eggs somewhere in a pan

there is a little girl studying for a math test at the kitchen table
her cereal sits tired
I take a picture of her house
the birds on the power lines
suddenly lift away
soundtrack for this morning would be piano in a cold room
muffled

I was small once too.

McDonald's more successful feature films have included Roadkill *(1989);* Highway 61 *(1991), for which he won Best Director at the highly regarded San Sebastián International Film Festival;* Dance Me Outside *(1994);* Hard Core Logo *(1996);* This Movie is Broken *(2010), featuring the band Broken Social Scene; and* Hard Core Logo II, *featuring singer Care Failure of the band Die Mannequin.* Roadkill *won Most Outstanding Canadian Film at the Toronto International Film Festival (TIFF), and* Hard Core Logo *has been frequently ranked amongst the greatest movies ever to come out of Canada. McDonald earned some notoriety when, while accepting his $25,000 prize from TIFF for* Roadkill, *he quipped that he planned to spend the money on "a big chunk of hash."*

GILLIAN:

the Tim Hortons sign, the cold pavement, the painted yellow line, the gravel, the mist

the cars passing

the cars passing

these thin slippers outdoors.

BRUCE:

I like broken

broken is so much more interesting to me than okay

I like not enough

I like not so much

in films when it looks as if it's broken or not right somehow but every single detail's been sweated out or recovered from something else – mined – every single thing right there where it's supposed to be – careful confusion – like the film was put in the camera upside down – but on purpose – everything all at once you know – and then one thing – so you focus in on that – but it's all one piece – art is just putting things together

five grams of hash and a green light

just because things look fucked up doesn't mean they actually are,

things are only fucked up if they're actually fucked up

beauty depends.

McDonald completed shooting The Tracey Fragments *(2006) in Toronto, which premiered at the Berlin International Film Festival. While shooting the scenes took him only two weeks, he spent nine months in post-production. The average length of human gestation is 280 days, or 40 weeks, or 9 months. There are many online pregnancy calculators for those who wish to confirm if they are pregnant.*

MID-
NIGHT
ALL
NIGHT

11

KEN CARTER

MORRISBURG, 1979

no one's ever done this before so there's no rules

no maps

for this

no way that it should be done or that it has to be done

this is the first time ever for this

ever

and you are here.

How do you develop an authentic voice for your point-of-view character? Here are some creative writing exercises to help. Writers and book reviewers talk about voice, developing a voice, or a novel or short story having an authentic voice. Editors look for voice in what they accept for publication. A writer develops his or her own voice through writing, writing, and writing some more. But beyond an author's own voice, the viewpoint character has a voice as well. When using a first person or limited third-person point of view, the narration in fiction is limited to what that character knows or sees. But the narrative itself is in the viewpoint character's own voice – his/her tone, word choices, attitude...

Gee I was out at the site today

things are coming along, the ramp looks just fine

they've still got that surface a little rough though

always something gets in the way you've just got to be so careful like that movie the other night was on

two fellas are talking and, they're just sitting there in a restaurant or something, and out of nowhere from up top comes this microphone on a stick you know, recording them, their voices, and I'm thinking, geez that's not right. So then I'm not watching a movie anymore I'm seeing these two guys pretending to be these other two guys and I'm just some guy sitting in a motel watching those guys and their microphone and I'm scratching my head and thinking do we ever do that? I don't mean in this movie here where you're filming me because the people out there, they know you're filming me, and there's a microphone right there recording my voice because I'm not pretending, you see

(reaches forward and touches camera lens with a finger)

This is me.

This is Ken Carter talking.

When I go up that ramp that's as real as it can get.

(sits back)

This is as real as it gets. This is me. There's nothing behind a curtain in our shows. There's a guy. There's a car. There's a ramp.

And there's the people too there's no show without the people I'm telling you that nothing short of a miracle is gonna stop me from goin' up that ramp.

There's no show without the people. There's no show without the show.

KEN CARTER CHARACTER NOTES:

Strength: Brave	*Related flaw: Can be foolhardy.*
Strength: Quick to act	*Related flaw: Often acts without thinking.*
Strength: Trusting	*Related flaw: Trusts the wrong people.*

People who get recognized do things that have never been done before and that's what I'm doing here. What I will do here. You wait and you'll see and you won't have to wait long it's happening

right

now.

THE VOICE IN FICTION:

In this section we investigate the relationship between narrative voice and authorial voice. It might be advisable in preparation to examine a text such as Herman Melville's Moby Dick *and consider at which points in the story the telling voice seems to be Ishmael's and at which points it seems more legitimately to belong to Melville himself? Other texts lending themselves to this type of examination might be Vladimir Nabokov's* Lolita *or, closer to home, Michael Ondaatje's* Coming Through Slaughter.

HE GRABBED HER SUDDENLY, HELD HER TO HIMSELF AND KISSED HER HARD LIKE IN A HOLLYWOOD MOVIE

11

GILLIAN SZE

MORRISBURG, 1999

the cows look abandoned against the fence

a plastic garbage bag hard pressed by the wind

the road stencilled with tire tracks

soft noses by the wire

everyone is wounded

when there is frost the footprints don't last long

and you can't always tell by looking at someone's face

where they've been

mud dried on their warm brown sides the cows come to the fence and

wait.

In this scene Gillian is contemplative, as if trying to decide what to do next. She takes a picture of the cows, pushes her hands into her pockets and turns.

Bruce is standing in the motel room with the telephone receiver to his ear. "Just tell him Bruce McDonald is calling him. Just tell him that."

Over his shoulder we can see Gillian through the window crossing the parking lot towards the motel room door. Bruce is unaware of her approach. He lights a cigarette, the phone now cradled to his ear by his shoulder. "Yeah, I'll wait. Yeah, well, everyone's waiting for something darlin'."

He exhales slowly.

BRUCE:

Well tell him I've got a gun to my head and I'll use it if he doesn't pick up the phone right now.

(The door opens and Gillian enters.)

BRUCE:

What? 'Course I don't really have a gun to my head. What do you think I am, a moron?

(He waves to Gillian who crosses the room and seems unsure which way to turn.)

BRUCE (still speaking into the phone):

You think I'm the kind of sucker to hold a gun to my own head?

(He drops the match he has been holding into an ashtray. He looks towards Gillian and shrugs, hands up as if to say, "What are you doing?" Gillian mouths the words, "I'm leaving." He speaks back to the phone.)

BRUCE:

Although if this takes much longer I may have to throw myself under a train.

(blocks the receiver with one hand)

BRUCE:

What do you mean you're leaving?

GILLIAN:

I mean I'm leaving. That's what 'I'm leaving' means – it means I'm leaving. Where are the keys?

BRUCE (speaking back into the receiver):

Honey, you ever seen a man get smeared by an oncoming train? You'll never eat chili again, I'll tell you that.

BRUCE (covering the receiver again and speaking now in a hushed tone):

That's crazy, you're leaving, you're not leaving... This is not a situation where you can just walk in and say I'm leaving and then leave...

GILLIAN:

Well, it's not a situation where I can stay, so...

(They both spot the car keys at the same time and make a dive for them. Bruce has to jump over the bed to do so and loses his balance, careening across the room. They both roll on the floor, struggling, Bruce still clutches the receiver from which we can hear a muffled voice.)

VOICE ON PHONE:

Mr. McDonald? I have your connection now. Mr. McDonald?

(They both have hold of the keys and continue to struggle on the floor.)

BRUCE:

Look, this is crazy, people don't just walk into a room and say I'm leaving.

GILLIAN:

I just did that.

BRUCE:

And then just walk out of the room and drive off in my fucking car. That's not what most people fucking do.

GILLIAN:

I'm not like most fucking people.

VOICE ON PHONE:

Mr. McDonald?

BRUCE:

I have to take this call.

GILLIAN:

Then take it.

(They both stop struggling.)

BRUCE:

You can't leave.

VOICE ON PHONE:

Mr. McDonald?

GILLIAN:

Let me have the keys or I'll jam your nuts so far up into your chest you'll need a flashlight and spelunking equipment just to find them.

(They stop struggling and watch each other's faces for a moment.)

BRUCE:

Just... wait 'til I take this call.

VOICE ON PHONE:

Mr. McDonald, I can hear you there.

GILLIAN:

Give me the keys and I'll wait.

(Bruce lets go of the keys and Gillian leaps up, making a run for the door. He follows but trips going through the door and hits the pavement hard.)

BRUCE (rolling):

Dammit Rocket!

(Gillian makes it to the car and climbs in, starts it up and accelerates quickly. Behind her through the rear window we see Bruce get to his feet and yell.)

BRUCE:

Rocket! Dammit! Dammit!

(Music: "Wipeout" by The Surfaris)

(Pull in on Gillian from her hands on the wheel to extreme close-up. Eyes. Smile. Cut to trunk interior.)

The gun. Her bag. A Molotov cocktail, rolling.

Extreme Close-Up ("ECU" or "XCU"): The shot is so tight that only a detail of the subject, such as someone's eyes, can be seen. Close-ups may be more expensive than other shots due to the extra lighting and makeup needed. Often they are used to show detail or to convey emotion. Depending on the importance of the shot to the film the use of the extreme close-up may actually be designated in the shooting script along with relevant characterization notes such as "Gillian is smiling and seems strangely elated."

MID-
NIGHT
ALL
NIGHT

12

KEN CARTER

MORRISBURG, 1979

remember ragged on the streets of Montreal no one knew me at home or anywhere else building a rocket from cardboard and sheet metal

on my way to anywhere away.

THRUST

The force that propels a rocket or spacecraft. Measured in pounds, kilograms or Newtons. Physically speaking, it is the result of pressure exerted on the wall of the combustion chamber.

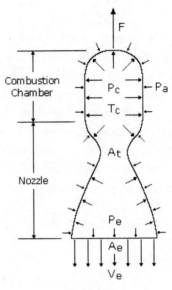

Figure 1.1

Figure 1.1 shows a combustion chamber with an opening (the nozzle) through which gas can escape. The force due to gas pressure on the bottom of the chamber is not compensated for from the outside. The resultant force (F) due to the internal and external pressure difference (the thrust) is opposite to the direction of the gas jet. It pushes the chamber upwards. Detailed studies would indicate that hydrogen propulsion is not ideally suited to a Lincoln Continental automobile and that sustained attention to such an effort could be indicative of delusional behaviour but not to any greater degree than the delusional or self-aggrandizing behaviour of many. We all of us once were children and with luck we may be again.

you can't do anything about the weather or much else

IMAGE
HAS GONE
MISSING

I have this memory it's stuck and it's my family like a painting in the old apartment in Montreal my daddy's at the table and my mother's making supper I guess and us kids are sitting on the couch, and I'm on the floor, and we're watching television, just getting dark and the snow falling is white in the black and swirling and those thin silvered window edges cold metal I remember it wasn't too long after this I had to leave — my mother calling to come to the table the smell of potatoes I loved my daddy I guess because he never left me let me ask you something since we're being pretty honest here you ever been making love to a woman and you both just start laughing and you can't stop? I mean, you can't stop fucking or laughing, either one?

somewhere now in the world it's snowing
now
and it's cold now.

In 1979 The Sugarhill Gang releases "Rapper's Delight." Built on a sample of Chic's disco hit "Good Times" and written by Grandmaster Caz of the Cold Crush Brothers, it goes on to become hip hop's first hit and mainstream America's first exposure to rap music. It has been seven years since DJ Hollywood, a club DJ from Manhattan, began rhyming over popular disco hits at trendy night spots. It is alleged that "Hollywood" coined the term 'hip hop,' though some say his partner, Lovebug Starski, came up with the term. Following the release of "Rapper's Delight," in order to capitalize on the growth of MCing in hip hop music, Grandmaster Flash recruits three of his friends — Keith "Cowboy" Wiggins, Melvin "Melle Mel" Glover, and Nathaniel "Kid Creole" Glover — to perform as an ensemble called Grandmaster Flash & the 3 MCs. Soon, they add Guy "Rahiem" Williams and Eddie "Scorpio" Morris, and change their name to "Grandmaster Flash and the Furious Five." After three more years, they release The Message, which moves away from hip hop's party-oriented singles, and instead, focuses on the realities of inner-city poverty and marks the first mainstream use of sampling; it is a landmark moment for hip hop.

they'll see and they'll know when I launch and I go / it's right here it's right on / light it up and I'm gone / don't care if they say can't be done won't be done / takes a badass to do this / no problem I'm one / dice is thrown stage is set / there's this way that I get / when I see what could be / but just hasn't been yet

and if that sounds like Seuss to you / see what I'll do to you / best way that I know that I can get through to you / is don't push me 'cause I'm close to the edge

I'm just trying not to lose my head

well it's never been done / let me tell you this son / just because you ain't done it / don't make it the one /thing that shouldn't be tried / let me pull you aside / let me tell you some truth / 'cause I haven't yet lied

it's not wise it's not brave just this thing that I do

but it's the one thing that keeps me from living like you

I got a Lincoln Continental and a sun-roofed Cadillac

and when I'm alone

that's when I feel it then the edge of the ramp

coming, just,

it's like that / and that's the way it is.

Sampling has been integral to hip hop production since its inception. In hip hop, the term describes a technique of splicing out or copying sections of other songs and rearranging or reworking these sections into a cohesive pattern.

HE GRABBED HER SUDDENLY, HELD HER TO HIMSELF AND KISSED HER HARD LIKE IN A HOLLYWOOD MOVIE

12

GILLIAN SZE

MORRISBURG, 1999

she's just driving but she's thinking too she thinks about well she thinks about driving and how far she can go and she thinks about all that she wants to do in the next fifty years or so and in the next five minutes and she thinks about the gun in the trunk

stops the car

and steps out onto the gravel shoulder it's colder now cars passing on highway two and she opens the trunk and stands looking at the pistol resting there on the brown carpeting picks it up

empties it, the bullets rattling out into the bowl of the spare tire puts it in her pocket pulls her hood up, pulls on the baggy pants she bought, big sunglasses

then hands   on the wheel
tight.

If you notice that a bank robbery is in progress, simply get some details on the robber that you can pass on to the police. Some helpful information: Clothing – look for layers under the visible layer (the outer layer will come off); physical characteristics – height, weight, eye colour, hair colour, mannerisms, scars/ tattoos; automobile description (not the most important since it's probably stolen); direction of travel; weapons – the police need to know if the robber is armed. Does the robber appear to be a poet or an artist of some kind? This is often the case. Police will need to know this.

The Ontario Provincial Police are seeking the public's assistance in identifying a man or woman believed to be responsible for a bank robbery in Morrisburg, Ontario on 30 October, 1999, at approximately 10:00 a.m. A hooded individual entered the bank and first appeared to write a note at the desk before quickly approaching the teller's counter with a drawn gun. The individual exited the bank with an undisclosed amount of cash and fled the scene in what appeared to be a black Dodge Charger. To assist with the investigation the Canadian Bankers Association is offering a $10,000 reward for information that leads to the arrest and conviction of the offender who is being referred to as the "Charger Bandit."

about dusk by the time she found the right field not close enough to anything that she'd be caught – not far enough away that she wouldn't find her way back on foot by morning she'd driven far she'd been surprised by how nervous she'd been when she walked into the bank covered up with clothes and hood and feeling naked she'd walked to the counter to write a note: I need as much money as you can get to me in thirty seconds something like that then all of a sudden she hadn't felt nervous and she decided to run at the teller with the gun pointed and yelling there'd been a woman and a man behind the counter and they'd both gone white she'd pulled the car over about ten minutes ago and there was more than fifty thousand dollars in the bag and she'd started shaking as she counted and it was a shame what she had to do now

There are many variations of the Molotov cocktail. The classic is a glass bottle filled with gasoline. An oil-soaked rag is placed in the neck of the bottle. The rag is lit on fire and the bottle is thrown at the opposition. However, practice has created new models of the Molotov that defeat the classic version. When making Molotovs, it is never a good idea to use the oily rag method. It can allow gas to seep from the bottle and many other bad things. The best way is to take a tampon that is soaked in gas and place it on the side of the bottle neck. Then, tie a rubber band around the tampon. Make sure the bottle has a cap on it. Light the tampon and throw hard.

tire crunch on gravel next and a yellow band low over the dark trees with the sun falling her footsteps on the flattened cornstalks metal slam of trunk she takes off the hoodie and slips into her leather jacket the pocket of which holds a knife which she uses to tear the sleeves now from the hoodie and then she ties them together places her bag on the ground next to the bottle lowers the sleeves into the gas tank to soak them and pulls them back out again and lets them drape plastered to the side of the car dries her hands on her pants looks around rubs her hands again and lights a cigarette smokes and then smiles reaches down and gentles the lighter up to the bottom of the sleeve only just a little surprised by how quick it takes she steps back quickly stumbling a bit and grabs her bag and bottle ready to throw in case the sleeves don't reach the gas ta--

EXT. - NIGHT

(A huge red fireball expands in silence behind Gillian as she walks calmly now in extreme slow motion towards the camera in silence, slowly filling the frame to a tight close-up on her face; a smile breaks open and a secondary explosion is heard mix to music intro:)

(Music: "Wipeout" by The Surfaris (reprise))

(fade to black)

driving to the field the early stars had hung in the night turning the sky like small white scraps of paper tied to the trees and she would go wherever she wanted now

nothing

could stop her. Sometimes the only way to finish one thing is to start something else.

The most highly explosive and lethal mixture is ammonium-nitrate–based fertilizer mixed with gasoline. Just stuff the bottle with this mixture and light the bastard. This method should be made with a plastic bottle so that it will not break on impact. When you light it, the bottle will quickly explode, so be quick. Using a fuse is a good idea.

Canada Council Withdrawal of Funding
Proposal/Application Information

Name: Bruce McDonald
Birthdate: May 28, 1959 (1959-05-28)
Place of Birth: Kingston, Ontario, Canada
Place of Residence: Toronto, Ontario, Canada
Nationality: Canadian
Occupation: Film Director
Title of Original Proposal: The Ken Carter Film

In twenty-five words or less provide a synopsis of the reasons for your withdrawal of the funding proposal/application:

Originally I had intended to make a film about the career of Ken Carter, the Canadian daredevil and car jumper. During the complicated process of on-site research I realized such a project may be unfeasible for a variety of logistical and emotional reasons. There were also some legal concerns which, although taxing, did not directly involve me. And I subsequently had a call regarding production of a film with Mickey Rourke which seems now to be green-lighted for production requiring me to attend meetings in Los Angeles later this week. So the Carter film seems to be on hold for now and likely for the foreseeable future. And there was also a problem with transportation.

Bitch blew up my car.

MID-
NIGHT
ALL
NIGHT

13

KEN CARTER

MORRISBURG, 1979

D'ya ever think about the number thirteen? About luck, and no luck? Shit, the rain we had that year would've held up the moon launch. We had to delay too many times and I knew the Hollywood producers were getting itchy about it. Itchy. They're itchy by nature. I knew it cost them twenty-five thousand a day but it could have cost me a hell of a lot more than that if we'd pushed it. Gloria always said she didn't like the feel of those guys ever, and I probably should have listened to her. LA cheap leather jackets. Well, I should have listened to her, let's be clear about that. And there I'm sitting in Room 1218 at the Four Seasons in Ottawa, we're in meetings there, and they send someone else in my car up my ramp while I'm not there... No. Someone who's not even qualified. He's a stuntman, he's a good stuntman, but he's not a driver. Obviously they shouldn't have done that.

This is not over. I will do that jump. It's back to where it started; a man, a car, just one man. Now I'm in it all by myself, a crowd full of spectators who come to see a man do his thing. I'm gonna get it done.

1 JULY, 2013

EXT. – TIM HORTONS – 6:14 P.M.

I'm waiting for a man named Howard Hudson at the Morrisburg Tim Hortons. On my second cup of coffee, a grey pickup rolls into the parking lot and he waves. It's raining lightly, like a mist, like it was on the day that Ken Carter's jump was postponed. The highway is a mirror.

"You Mike?" he asks, his window rolling down as I walk out.

"You want a coffee?" I ask.

"No, thanks."

We shake hands.

"Howard," he says.

Just then a black Charger pulls into the lot, its exhaust a low rumble. We both pause to watch. A blond-haired kid comes out of the coffee shop and watches the car roll up to the curb.

"Well, let's go," Howard says.

He's agreed to take me to the jump site, or whatever's left of the jump site, which, according to our phone conversation, isn't much.

"You wouldn't even know it's there if you didn't know it's there, if you know what I mean," he'd said.

It's later in the day now than I had planned and I'm worried that the evening light will not be enough to see by.

"I'll take you out Lakeshore first – you'll see the ramp they built, I mean the place where they built it, they took it down a long time ago… There's not much left to see."

Over the phone I'd learned that Howard worked for Hydro, lived in Morrisburg and yes, he had been there the day of the jump – though for a while I hadn't been sure if he'd meant one of the days the jump was aborted by Carter and his crew or the day the producers had replaced Carter with Kenny Powers and the jump had gone ahead.

"This rain should have passed over by now; they'll want it clear by the time they shoot those fireworks tonight. We'll probably head out on the boat later to see them."

We pass houses by the water, and pull up by a stop sign.

"Did you meet him?" I ask.

Howard's watching the opposite corner where a kid is waiting with a bike. He waves the kid across.

"I should probably watch what I say... People around here didn't think that much of him really. I mean, by the end, this had gone on for a few years. Nobody thought it was going to happen by the end."

The kid hops back onto his bike. There's a baseball or hockey card folded into the spokes for the noise. Old-school.

We're heading into space that I recognize from YouTube and Google.

"Here we go."

Howard slows down a bit, the four-ways clicking, rain hitting the windshield.

"That white house would have been here back then, not these others. The ramp was over there. It was quite something, 'bout three storeys up. I can take you up onto Number Two and you can see where the track started."

He turns around slowly with one hand on the wheel, neck turned hard, the leather seat crunching.

"You see where all these house trailers are, they weren't here then either. If you drive down there you can see a stretch of the old highway from before they flooded the river..."

"Were there many people?"

"That day, no. We'd heard so many times, 'Kenny's going today. He's doin' 'er' that people just stopped showing up. I headed out here though. 'Course it wasn't Ken Carter, they'd put the other fella into 'er. We didn't know that then. There you go."

He's pulling over again and flipping the four-ways back on.

"I'll just back up."

He checks and slowly reverses on the shoulder.

"There."

He nods his head at a corner of a field.

"We were lined up along here. Not too many cars. Maybe twenty people."

We sit looking at the grass in the field. Two cars and a truck pass.

"Right there. Off he went."

I imagine the blast of the rocket and the smell and the car ripping suddenly away towards the ramp.

"Crazy as shit though. Wow. All history now."

Sheet metal tearing off as it leaves the ramp. Vapour trail parachute.

"Is that what this book's about?" he asks, windshield wipers

quietly

quietly sweeping

something about to happen, and I don't move

the sky here the same as anywhere else.

END.

SOME POSTSCRIPTS

th keep going part uv us can b
invinsibul

                    until its not

– bill bissett

Everything is biographical, Lucian Freud says. What we make, why it is made, how we draw a dog, who it is we are drawn to, why we cannot forget. Everything is collage, even genetics. There is the hidden presence of others in us, even those we have known briefly. We contain them for the rest of our lives, at every border we cross.

– MICHAEL ONDAATJE

THE CAST

MICHAEL BLOUIN'S critically acclaimed first novel, *Chase and Haven* (2008), was a finalist for the Amazon First Novel Award and won the 2009 ReLit Award for Best Novel. In 2007 his first collected poetry *I'm not going to lie to you* (2007) was a finalist for the Lampman Award. In 2011 Pedlar Press released *Wore Down Trust*, which won the 2012 Lampman Award. He was a finalist for the 2010 CBC Literary Awards and his work has been published in many literary magazines, including *Descant, Arc, Branch, Dragnet, The Antigonish Review, Event, Grain, Queen's Quarterly, The New Quarterly*, and *The Fiddlehead*. He is represented internationally by Westwood Creative Artists.

BRUCE MCDONALD is the foremost independent film director in Canada. His films include *Traplines* (1986), *Roadkill* (1989), *Highway 61* (1991), for which he won Best Director at the San Sebastián International Film Festival, *Dance Me Outside* (1994), *Hard Core Logo* (1996), *Picture Claire* (2001) (with Mickey Rourke), *The Tracey Fragments* (2006), *Pontypool* (2009) and *This Movie is Broken* (2010). *Roadkill* won Most Outstanding Canadian Film at the Toronto International Film Festival and *Hard Core Logo* has been frequently ranked amongst the greatest movies ever to come out of Canada. 2012 saw the release of *Hard Core Logo II*, featuring Care Failure and the band Die Mannequin.

GILLIAN SZE is the author of *Peeling Rambutan* (forthcoming 2014) and *The Anatomy of Clay* (2011). Her debut poetry collection, *Fish Bones* (2009), was shortlisted for the 2009 QWF McAuslan First Book Prize. She is the co-founder and co-editor of *Branch Magazine* and teaches creative writing to youth. Gillian has a Master of Arts degree in Creative Writing from Concordia University and is currently working on a PhD at Université de Montréal.

ACKNOWLEDGE-
MENTS

I would like to extend my gratitude to the following people for making what I do easier:

Deborah Rutherford, Mary Newberry, Jay MillAr and Hazel Millar, Beth Follett, Sandra Ridley, Chris Casuccio, Hilary McMahon, Alana Wilcox, Sean and Neil Wilson, bill bissett, Lynn Crosbie, Susan Musgrave, David Francey and rob mclennan, as well as to Arc Poetry Magazine for many years of support and encouragement.

And to Gillian Sze, Bruce McDonald, and Howard Hudson for their involvement and for allowing themselves to be fictionalized for this book without asking for any editorial input. Thanks for passing through. Many thanks also to Gillian for her graciousness in permitting the use of her images.

Bruce McDonald: http://www.shadowshows.com/

Gillian Sze: http://www.gilliansze.com/

MUSIC:

The playlist for this book was:

Matthew Maaskaant: "Fall To Pieces"
Die Mannequin: "Danceland"
The Hylozoists: "Soixante-Neuf"
Mark Haney: "Aim for the Roses"
Justin Townes Earle: "Harlem River Blues"
Neil Young: "I Was Born in Ontario"

SOME ADDITIONAL WEB VOICES:

The ramp and its runway were located in a field just west of Hanes Road, south of County Road 2 in Morrisburg, Ontario, Canada. On the Canadian side, it is between Carowan Road to the west and Hanes Road to the east. If you use Google Maps (satellite view), find Ogden Island (on the US side of the St. Lawrence River) and pan across to Canada. You can still see the remnants of the runway (on high magnification). Alternatively, search the following coordinates on Google Maps: 44.882900,-75.217102

I lived on Muttonville Road, not even a half-kilometre northeast of this. I faintly remember watching this from the top of our house. I was able to get my picture taken with the car at the wrecking yard (Norm McIntosh) after they towed it out of the river. No matter what people thought of Ken Carter, it took balls to do something like this. Love him or hate him, I think some sort of memorabilia should be posted somewhere. I wish they would have left the ramp standing!!!!

Welcome to the Morrisburg Google Satellite Map! This place is situated in Stormont, Ontario, Canada. Its geographical coordinates are 44° 54' 0" North, 75° 11' 0" West and its original name (with diacritics) is Morrisburg. See Morrisburg photos and images from satellite below, explore the aerial photographs of Morrisburg in Canada. Morrisburg hotels map is available on the target page linked above.

SOME FAVOURITE STORIES FROM RALPH HURLEY:

Ken Carter, the legendary Canadian stuntman, was booked by Hurley for a special show on a race night at Cornwall Motor Speedway. Carter was to drive a car off a ramp and over twenty-two cars... at least that was the game plan. As the stuntman's crew put the cars from a local wrecker in place, Carter challenged Hurley to put his vehicle in the number fifteen slot. Hurley, without much thought, said okay. His recently purchased two-year-old New Yorker was put in the number fifteen spot, considered a pretty safe place since Carter routinely jumped twenty cars. At the number four turn, Carter revved up his high-powered car as Hurley watched from the infield, puffing on a cigarette. The stunt car came barrelling down the straightaway in front of the grandstand, up on the ramp and just as it was at maximum speed about five feet from the top, a rear tire blew. The car left the ramp and came down hard on the roof of Hurley's car. Hurley stood in the infield trying to believe what he had just witnessed. The crowd, of course, thought it was great. Most of the fans thought it was part of the act. Hurley wanted to cry. His wife wanted to kill him. The word was that Carter paid for the car.

He had kahunas as big as a fist... Note the lack of safety gear amongst other things. This was done at the racetrack that was a short distance from where I lived back in 1976 when racing cars were still real cars. The track has since closed and is now a waterslide/mini-putt park.

...Really can't believe with all the car guys here, we don't have more input on this guy.

I am looking for anyone with photos of stuntman Ken Carter. He would jump twelve to sixteen cars (with a white Nova or Impala) at local short tracks in the northeast in the mid-70s. I am specifically looking for any photos from Fulton Speedway in Fulton, NY. Fulton was pavement back at that time and is now dirt. I was between eight to ten years old at the time, so I am sorry I do not have a specific date. Our family car, a mid-60s gold Bonneville was near the end of the landing. My dad raced a hobby Stock 57 Chevy back in the day and has since passed away. This photo will help re-live those fun days at the track. I have an internet photo of Ken Carter but I do not know how to post it here. If anyone thinks they have what I am looking for I can send it to them. Thanks.

Here is a car guy that followed his dream to the end.

Ken Carter once said:

"I'm looking for the ultimate statement,
Ken Carter, World's Greatest Daredevil."

Ken Carter (1938–September 5, 1983), born Kenneth Gordon Polsjek,
was a Canadian stunt driver. In 1983 he attempted to jump a pond in
Peterborough, Ontario. During the jump, his car – a modified Pontiac
Firebird – had a malfunction and Carter crashed badly but vowed to
try the jump again. Several months later, he did. The vehicle missed
its target landing ramp by thirty metres and landed on its roof.
Carter was killed instantly. He is buried in an unmarked grave
in the Notre-Dame-des-Neiges Cemetery in Montreal.

THANKS FOR THE RIDE, KEN.

OTHER BOOKS BY MICHAEL BLOUIN:

Chase and Haven
I'm not going to lie to you
Wore Down Trust

COLOPHON:

Manufactured as the first edition of
I Don't Know How To Behave
in the Fall of 2013 by BookThug.

Distributed in Canada by
the Literary Press Group:
www.lpg.ca

Distributed in the United States by
Small Press Distribution:
www.spdbooks.org

Shop on-line at www.bookthug.ca

BOOK
PRODUCTION
WAR ECONOMY
STANDARD

Text + design by Jay MillAr
Copy edited by Ruth Zuchter